Funny Bone Readers™

Response to Bullying

HOW TO DEAL WITH BULLIES
SUPERHERO STYLE

by Wiley Blevins • illustrated by Debbie Palen

RED CHAIR
·PRESS·

Please visit our website at **www.redchairpress.com**.
Find a free catalog of all our high-quality products for young readers.

Publisher's Cataloging-In-Publication Data
(Prepared by The Donohue Group, Inc.)

Blevins, Wiley.
    How to deal with bullies superhero style : response to bullying / by Wiley Blevins ;
illustrated by Debbie Palen. -- [First edition].

    pages : illustrations ; cm. -- (Funny bone readers. Dealing with bullies)

    Summary: Zach is a kid just like you and me, but when Zach sees others being teased
or bullied, he imagines himself as a superhero and comes to the rescue. With powerful
words like "No teasing! No hitting! That's just wrong!," Zach helps his friends learn to
use words for good and not to fight back or say mean things. Includes glossary, as well
as questions to self-check comprehension.
    Interest age level: 004-008.
    Edition statement supplied by publisher.
    Issued also as an ebook.
    ISBN: 978-1-63440-009-1 (library hardcover)
    ISBN: 978-1-63440-010-7 (paperback)

    1. Boys--Juvenile fiction. 2. Superheroes--Juvenile fiction. 3. Bullying--Juvenile
fiction. 4. Assertiveness in children--Juvenile fiction. 5. Boys--Fiction. 6. Superheroes--
Fiction. 7. Bullying--Fiction. 8. Assertiveness (Psychology)--Fiction. I. Palen, Debbie.
II. Title. III. Title: Superhero style

PZ7.B618652 Ho 2015
[E]   2014958273

This series first published by:
Red Chair Press LLC   PO Box 333   South Egremont, MA 01258-0333

Printed in the United States of America

042015 1P WRZF15

Zach is a kid just like you.
At least on the weekends.
But during the week, he's a . . .

SUPERHERO!

On Monday, Zach spots a bully.
He's making fun of a kid.
"Hold on," says Zach.

Zach pulls on his tights.
He throws on his mask and cape.
He rushes in.

NO TEASING

NO TAUNTING

NO CALLING NAMES

The only name you can call someone
is the name their mom gave them.

On Tuesday, Zach spots another bully.
He's hitting a boy.
"I'll be right there," says Zach.

8

Zach pulls on his tights.
He throws on his mask and cape.
He rushes in.

And only bite your sandwiches!

10

On Wednesday, Zach spots a new bully.
She's not letting a girl play with the group.
"Not cool," says Zach.

Zach pulls on his tights.
He throws on his mask and cape.
He rushes in.

NO HURTING OTHERS

NO LEAVING KIDS OUT

EVERYONE CAN PLAY

There's always room for one more.

On Thursday, Zach spots another bully.
He's scaring a little boy.
"Not on my watch," says Zach.

14

Zach pulls on his tights.
He throws on his mask and cape.
He rushes in.

Hurting someone to feel good about yourself never ends well.

On Friday, Zach spots one last bully.
She's telling lies about someone.
"I hate those stories," says Zach.

Zach pulls on his tights.
He throws on his mask and cape.
He rushes in.

Use your words for good
and good is what you'll get back.

19

"Thanks," said all the kids Zach saved.
"We don't know what we'd do
without you."

"You can do what I do," said Zach.

20

"But never fight, cry, or say mean things," said Zach. "Most bullies like that. Do you think you can do it?"

Big Questions: What can you do or say when a bully bothers you? Does Zach say you should say mean things back to a bully? Why or why not?

Big Words:

bully: a person who harms others with mean words or actions